P9-BYN-051

The Adventures of
PETOSKEY STONE
MALONE

The Adventures of
PETOSKEY STONE
MALONE

Written and Illustrated by *Dub McPeak*

No part of this publication may be reproduced, stored in a retrieval system, or transmitted in any form or by any means, electronic, mechanical, photocopying, recording, or otherwise, without written permission of the author. For information regarding permission, email requests to petoskeystonemalone@gmail.com

ISBN 978-0-615-49001-4

Text and illustrations copyright © 2011 by Kathleen Mavourneen Jacobsen.
All rights reserved.

www.petoskeystonemalone.com

Printed by Sheridan Press in Ann Arbor, Michigan

The images in this book are a melding of hand-drawn ink sketches, watercolor painting, and digital photography.

Thanks to my daughter Audrey and my mother Marguerite for their help with illustrations. Thanks to my son Alexander for endlessly listening to Malone's story and loving him as much as I do. Thanks to my husband Ragnar for all his encouragement during the writing of this book. Finally, I would like to thank Tamra Bell for her graphic design expertise — you have all played an important role in bringing Malone's story to life.

— Kathleen (Dub McPeak) Jacobsen

TABLE OF CONTENTS

There is a place where the **beachcombers** roam,
where the stones have eyes as hard as your bones.

There is one stone that stands out, he is quite **particular**;
when he lay in the sun, he lay **perpendicular**.

His name is Malone, and this is his home;
the bright shores of a bay, that glisten like **chrome**.

One day he was picked up, near the **Old Tannery**,
by a man out walking, Mr. O'Flannery.
Now Mr. O'Flannery, or Jim as he's known,
had passed by here often as he liked to skip stones.
Malone was concerned that *he too* would be thrown.
Rather, the man held him tightly and headed for home.

Jim was about to ship out, he was in the **Navy**.
There was a vast war being fought, his job **"wouldn't be gravy."**

At first, everything was very exciting.

They were always searching for those they were fighting.

But, it was the evenings that Malone was mostly **delighting**.
The sea **swaying** nights were filled with **reciting**
and the earthy smell from the pencils when Jim did his writing.

Malone is what's called a "worry stone."
Worry Stones are meant to be rubbed, they're meant to be held,
they're meant to be loved.
When this doesn't happen, their skin, it starts **chapping**.
It's the oil from your hands they're supposed to be **lapping**.

Jim had **"shore leave"** but just for the day.
That meant leaving the ship; He went to **Hanauma Bay**.
It was Hawaii's best place to see fish, but not for the serving dish.
Rather, the **tropical type** all covered in stripes.

Jim brought with him some old dried peas.
He had heard that the fish really like these.
As Jim waded in, all the fish and their **kin**
swam right to his pockets. They were as fast as rockets.
A **parrotfish** mistook Malone for a pea,
something that Jim did not **foresee**.
He was narrowly rescued just as a wave crested.
If it hadn't been for Jim he'd a been **ingested**.

Malone liked to sit on the **porthole** sill.

The view was always best here, but today he felt **ill**.

The waves were making the ship really **sway**.

He slid for a time… then fell…

to **Pearl Harbor Bay**.

As he was falling, he heard a bird calling,
to her tight little **brood** out looking for food.
Malone aimed towards them, landing in feathers...
on the back of a **Nene**, now safely **tethered**.

They swam for bit, then the bird began **chiding**
and pecking her wing where Malone had been hiding.
With her strong blackened beak, Malone was then tweaked
and tossed like a ball to a bright **coral** wall.

On this **reef** Malone was sad and missed the old days with Jim,
and the shores of the bay where he had met him.
He *did* love the games with the **cauliflower coral**.
They were very quick-witted, and looked almost **floral**.

Eventually, he was plucked up without any warning;
by a curious gull out early one morning.
With this **scavenger** bird, he flew over **Diamond Head Crater**,
over **Waikiki**, over the fancy **waiter**.

He dropped right smack down into a **plumeria lei**;
that **swaddled** him in fragrance and carried him away.

The **tourist** he rode was warm like the ocean.
She was red as a crab and smelled of coconut lotion.
She was boarding a plane bound for the **mainland**,
soaring away, with bright travelers on hand.

Up in the clouds with this strange-seated crowd;
each one buckled tight, he'd never seen such a sight.
The lady whose **lei** he rode, her name was Gertrude.
She was eating some **poi**… it looked sort of pre-chewed.

Next to the window was a man and his bride.
They were both gazing thoughtfully into some type of guide.
It told of a museum **brimming** with fossils.
Just then, old Gert started to **jostle**.

From this side of Gert, the view was quite **varied**.

For where did the couple go who had just been married?

A paper was peaking from under Gert's iced tea.

It was a homebound ticket; it read "Destination D.C."

Malone had no plan… things were going so fast,

It was the role of "adventurer" that he had been cast.

His airplane now **grounded**, Malone was **confounded**
everyone began standing, this group was **disbanding**.
All this was too much for his understanding.
Then, Gert discovered some food stuck to her **molar**.
When she tried to **dislodge** it, Malone fell to a stroller.

This **buggy** was sticky, yet soft and still picky.
There were all types of crumbs and babies sucking their thumbs.
He felt overwhelmingly prickly and was moving quite quickly,
with the **unswerving** mother, of this sister and brother.

Outside it was snowing... the cold wind was blowing.
How would he ever see where he was going?
The answer to this question, his **fate** was **prolonging**
all squished up and folded with this family's belongings.

When at last they unloaded, out he **exploded**!
Inside, he felt as if something **imploded**.
It was his heart; he could feel every last flutter.
He bounced, rolled, and then stopped, just short of a **gutter**.

It was a very good thing that the road had been salted.

For this is the reason that he had been **halted**.

He sat for a while, then a little while longer.

There was some answer here, he just had to think stronger.

It was the five o'clock rush,
the streets were all jammed and filled with cold mush.
Those coming at him were wearing dark suits.
Some **tread** grabbed him right up to one of their boots.
So, it was like this he traveled stuck to a **galosh**;
step-click, step-click through the cold winter slosh.

After some time he felt something **prying**,
to **dislodge** him frantically someone was trying.
A man was coughing and clearing his throat.
Just then, he was placed into a warm **cashmere** coat.

He dried surrounded by **lint** and receipts.
It was a much better way to travel these streets.

Some time passed, he knew… probably weeks,
then came the sound of laughter and **shrieks**.
A hand reached into the pocket… this time smaller.
The child whose hand it was started to holler.
She was squealing with happiness at her discovery.
Malone was relieved at his **recovery**.
Lulu showed Malone to her brothers.
They both begged to hold him one after the other.

He slept that night in the softness of cotton…
his **harrowing** trip almost forgotten.

When he awoke, Malone wasn't the same.

I guess you could say that he felt very strange.

Somehow this child's **affection** had changed his **complexion**.

He was covered in stickers… her entire collection!

With her, he enjoyed his very own mansion.
A bed his own size, and a room just for dancing.
Whenever he was hurt or just somewhat sad,
Lulu showed him **compassion**, all that she had.

Now, Leo and Mike played quite a bit rougher.

Malone liked this change... a chance to feel tougher.

With them he rode in a dump truck bright yellow.

Got sandy, got dirty, got covered in Jell-O.

So, it was like this he spent the rest of the winter.

With a family he loved and their **Doberman Pinscher**.

When spring came and the landscape bred wonder and **astonishment**;
the family had a picnic near the **Washington Monument**.
As their lunch was **devoured**, the **cherry blossoms** showered,
over Malone and the others for over an hour.

Malone and this clan of **Washingtonians**
loved the museums of the **Smithsonian**.
In the first place they stopped they saw a flag named **"Old Glory."**
They viewed **Lincoln**'s Hat, and learned his life story.

First Ladies' Dresses

But, Lulu confessed that the room she loved best,
was where the First Ladies' forms were so elegantly dressed.
Their gowns were **adorned** with silk, jewels, and lace.
She could almost touch them... if not for the glass case.

But, Leo and Mike by the looks on their faces,
definitely wanted to see other places.

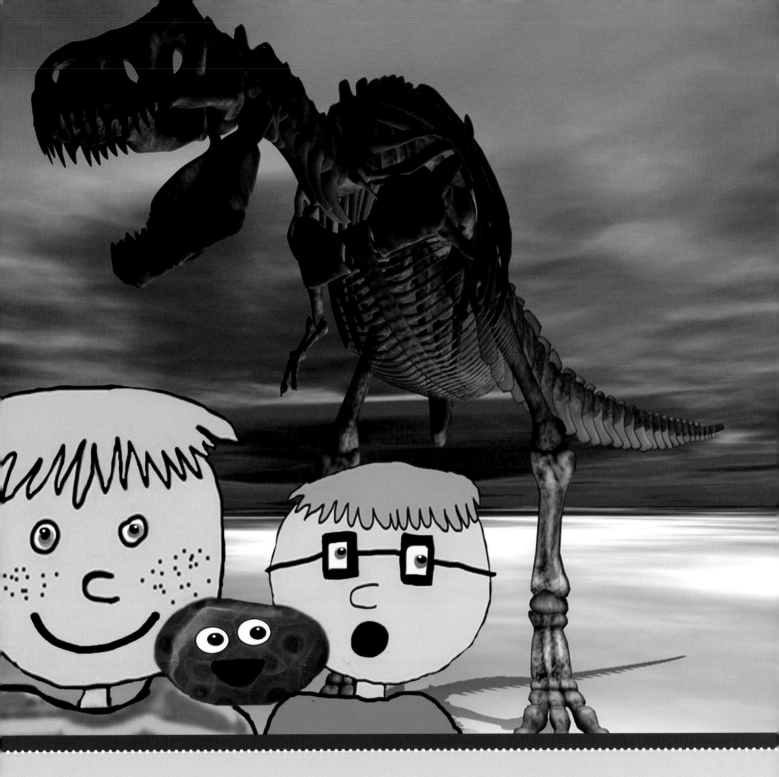

What they loved the best, not that they disliked the rest...
was where the dinosaurs were, that was for sure!
They saw **raptors** that captured their **prey** with their feet.
They saw dinos who preferred not to eat any meat.
Then, in the **Devonian** section, there was a collection called "Coral in Disguise,"
which **boasted** fossils with eyes.

OSSILS WITH EYES
Hexagonaria Percarinata

DEVONIAN PERIOD

Petoskey
Michigan

They saw stones like Malone called, **Hexagonaria Percarinata**.

Here he would not be **"persona non grata".**

He was once a colony of live coral, they learned.

Bright and bold, to know more they **yearned**;

with **tentacles** of red, from which he once fed, millions of years ago;

that's what it said. In Northern Michigan, they soon uncovered;

is where stones like Malone are mostly discovered.

Malone, the stone many times **displaced**,
was somehow famous in this place.

Observing Malone in this very new light,
each one asked to hold him, each one held him tight.
His past now **revealed**... no longer **concealed**,
with this wonderful family his **fate** had been sealed.

If you're ever so lucky, to find a friend like Malone;
Love him and take him on adventures all your own.
But, never let him forget, **Petoskey's Little Traverse Bay**,
where each year the **beachcombers** still return to this day.

Glossary

A

Adorned: Decorated
Affection: Love
Astonishment: Surprise

B

Beachcombers: People who walk near the water looking for stones or shells
Boasted: To brag
Brimming: Overflowing
Brood: Family
Buggy: Baby Stroller

C

Cashmere: Warm wool made from goat hair
Cauliflower coral: A type of ocean coral that resembles the vegetable cauliflower
Chapping: When skin becomes dry and flaky
Cherry Blossoms: Flowers that grow into cherries, commonly found around the Monuments in Washington, D.C., and in and around Traverse City, Michigan, the Cherry Capital
Chiding: To scold
Chrome: A type of shiny metal
Compassion: Kindness
Complexion: Facial appearance or skin tone
Concealed: Hidden
Confounded: Confused
Coral: A rock-like group of certain sea animals or their skeletons that form a reef

D

Delighting: Enjoying
Devonian: A geologic period of the Paleozoic Era about 416 to 359 million years ago when the live coral that is now the Petoskey Stone existed
Devoured: To eat very quickly and completely
Diamond Head Crater: An inactive volcano that is popular place to hike in the Waikiki region of Honolulu, Hawaii
Disbanding: To scatter or spread out

Dislodge: To remove or force out from a position or dwelling previously occupied
Displaced: Moved or relocated
Doberman Pinscher: A specific breed of dog

·· E / F ··

Exploded: To burst out
Fate: As used here, refers to Malone's future
Floral: Flowery, or flower-like
Foresee: To predict

·· G ··

Galosh: A rubber boot
Grounded: Landed on the ground
Gutter: Sewer grate

·· H ··

Halted: Stopped
Hanauma Bay: An inactive volcanic crater in Honolulu, Hawaii that is a great place to snorkel and see brightly colored tropical fish
Harrowing: Upsetting
Hexagonaria Percarinata: The scientific name for the Petoskey Stone, the state stone of Michigan

·· I ··

Ill: To feel sick
Implode: To burst inward
Ingested: To eat something

·· J / K ··

Jostle: To move around
Kin: Family, relatives

·· L ··

Lapping: Drinking
Lei: A necklace of traditionally live flowers worn on special occasions, especially in Hawaii

Lincoln: The 16th president of the United States known for freeing the slaves and his tall top hat

Lint: The fluffy stuff often found at the bottom of pockets or in belly buttons

Little Traverse Bay: A small body of water off Lake Michigan in the Northern Lower Peninsula of Michigan, the cities of Petoskey and Harbor Springs are on this bay

·· M ··

Mainland: What people living in Hawaii call the connected 48 states (excludes Alaska and Hawaii)

Molar: A type of large tooth at the back of the mouth

·· N ··

Nene: The state bird of Hawaii

Navy: The sea-faring branch of the United States Military

·· O ··

Observing: To look at very closely, to examine

"Old Glory": A nickname for the flag whose "broad stripes and bright stars" inspired Francis Scott Key to write a song that eventually became the United States National Anthem

Old Tannery: A factory no longer in existence, once on the shores of Little Traverse Bay in the Kegomic region of Petoskey that processed animal hides and turned them into leather

·· P ··

Parrotfish: A type of tropical fish whose coloring and head resembles the parrot-type bird

Particular: Picky

Pearl Harbor Bay: A lagoon harbor west of Honolulu, Hawaii and the headquarters for the United States Pacific Naval Fleet

Perpendicular: Up at a 90-degree angle

"Persona non grata": Latin for "an unwelcome person"

Petoskey: A city and coastal resort community located on the shores of Little Traverse Bay and a great place to find Petoskey Stones like Malone

Plumeria: A type of tropical flower that smells really nice

Poi: A popular food staple in the Polynesian/Hawaiian diet, made from the root of the taro plant

Porthole sill: The window area of a boat or ship

Prey: An animal taken by a predator as food

Prolonging: To make longer or lengthen in regards to time

Prying: To loosen or remove an object using another object

.... R ....

Raptors: A bird-like dinosaur

Reciting: To speak or recite poetry or other literary works

Recovery: In this case, to be rescued

Revealed: Uncovered, known

Reef: A ridge of coral at or near the surface of the ocean

.... S ....

Scavenger: Describes a particular type of animal or bird who eats almost anything

Shore leave: A naval term meaning to have permission to leave the ship to do fun things

Shrieks: Screams

Smithsonian: A Federal complex in Washington, D.C. with many free and interesting museums

Soaring: Flying

Swaddled: To be tightly wrapped up in something as Malone was in flowers

Sway / Swaying: To move from side to side

.... T ....

Tentacles: Narrow, flexible, parts extending from the body of certain animals

Tethered: To be joined or connected to something

Tourist: Someone who is on vacation

Tread: The grooved part of a shoe or boot that touches the ground

Tropical: Describes a hot climate or region near the equator

·· U / V ··

Unswerving: In this case, won't get out of the way for others

Varied: Different

·· W / Y ··

Waiter: A male who brings food to people eating in a restaurant

Waikiki: A neighborhood of Honolulu, Hawaii with Waikiki Beach and Diamond Head Crater

Washingtonians: A nickname for people who live in Washington, D.C.

Washington Monument: A 555-foot obelisk-shaped monument in Washington, D.C. built in honor of the first president of the United States, George Washington

"Wouldn't be gravy": An expression meaning that it "wouldn't be easy"

Yearned: To want something very much

Malone's Petoskey Scones

Ingredients:

- 2 ½ cups All Purpose Flour
  (*Malone prefers using 1¼ cup whole wheat flour and 1¼ cup white flour, Leo likes white flour only*)
- ½ teaspoon salt
- ½ cup sugar
- 2 teaspoons baking powder double acting

- 10 tablespoons unsalted butter
- ¾ cup half and half or whole milk
- 1 large egg + 1 large egg yolk
- chocolate chips or blueberries to place on outside of scone as the "eyes"
- coarse white sanding sugar for sprinkling

Directions:

Preheat the oven to 400°F. Lightly grease (or line with parchment) a baking sheet.

In a medium-sized bowl, whisk together the flour, salt, sugar, and baking powder till thoroughly combined. Add the butter, working it in with a large fork until the mixture is unevenly crumbly.

Whisk together the cream or milk and whole egg. Add to the dry ingredients and mix just long enough to form moist dough.

Transfer the sticky dough to a heavily floured work surface. Gently press dough to about a 1-inch thickness. Cut scones out using a 2-inch biscuit cutter making sure to dip the biscuit cutter in flour frequently; Malone says that you'll have to gather the scraps and reshape the dough at least once. Space the scones evenly on the prepared pan.

Brush with beaten large egg yolk, sprinkle heavily with coarse sugar, and decorate generously with chocolate chips or blueberries. If using chocolate chips, press the pointed end into the dough. Mike likes creating different patterns with both blueberries and chocolate making the Petoskey Scone look like a real Petoskey Stone.

>> *Family tip: Malone prefers semi-sweet chips while Lulu prefers 60% Cacao chips.*

Bake the scones for 13 minutes or until they're light golden brown. Remove them from the oven, and serve warm with an ice-cold glass of milk.   MAKES ABOUT 30 SMALL SCONES

Don't forget to share with your favorite Petoskey Stone!

Dedicated in memory of the real Sailor Jim, Professor James L. McPeak and his son, Michael Seamus "Peaker" McPeak.

Pictured above are the real Sailor Jim, Lulu (Dub McPeak), and Mike.